T0196317

TRUE BELIEVER

TRUE BELIEVER

Rape at Fort Bliss

PAUL BOUCHARD

TRUE BELIEVER
RAPE AT FORT BLISS

iUniverse books may be ordered through booksellers or by contacting:

iUniverse
1663 Liberty Drive
Bloomington, IN 47403
www.iuniverse.com
1-800-Authors (1-800-288-4677)

ISBN: 978-1-4917-8677-2 (sc)
ISBN: 978-1-4917-8676-5 (e)

Library of Congress Control Number: 2016901641

Print information available on the last page.

iUniverse rev. date: 06/02/2016

For the True Believers and Government Hacks

CHAPTER ONE

"Accused and defense counsel, please rise," said Judge Cohen. Captains Mark Sanders and Jacob Epstein rose to their feet, as did their client, who was sandwiched between them.

"Sergeant Keyshawn Adams. This court-martial sentences you to twenty-five years confinement, to be reduced to the rank of E-1 private, and to be dishonorably discharged from the army. Please be seated."

Cohen, a twenty-three-year army veteran and a full-bird colonel, cleared his throat with a short cough. "Are there any other matters to take up, counsel?"

"No," said both the prosecuting trial counsel, Captain Andrew Ford, and the lead defense counsel, Captain Sanders.

"Very well," Cohen said. "This court-martial is adjourned."

CHAPTER TWO

Christ, thought Sanders as he drove his Honda Civic west on I-10 heading home. It was eight o'clock on a Friday night, and it was still bright out. Traffic was moderate. He had the cruise control set at sixty-five miles per hour.

Damn. Twenty-five years. It was the harshest sentence ever imposed on one of his clients.

He passed the University of Texas at El Paso to his right, and to his left, directly across the narrow and shallow-water Rio Grande River, was one of Juarez, Mexico's, poorest neighborhoods.

Twenty-five frigging years, he thought. He reached down with his right hand for his venti cup of Starbucks. He took a sip. *There's truth to the saying that the toughest cases are the ones where you believe your client.*

Keyshawn Adams had indeed maintained his innocence for the brutal rape of his on-again, off-again girlfriend, twenty-five-year-old Sonia Martinez. The prosecution had offered a plea deal to Adams: plead guilty, and the jail time would be capped at ten years. But the twenty-five-year-old sergeant wouldn't budge; he was adamant he hadn't raped Martinez.

Sanders reached El Paso's last western exit and took a sharp left. The red-rock Franklin Mountains were to his right, and straight ahead was a huge truck stop and New Mexico with its flat, expansive landscape.

Martinez was a true victim—there was no doubting that. On the night of the crime, there had been a party for Adams's twenty-fourth birthday. Lots of people. Lots of booze and drugs. Lots of sex too. Martinez had been drinking heavily that night, and earlier in the evening, she had broken up with Sergeant Adams for the "final" time, something she was prone to do because of his constant infidelity.

Also not in dispute was the fact the recently broken-up couple had had sex that evening, the "one more time before we call it quits" kind of sex. But later that night, after many beers, numerous strawberry daiquiris, and countless drinks from a massive punch bowl that consisted of who knows what, Martinez found herself drunk and in and out of consciousness, in a blur, a haze, unsure of her surroundings. Next thing she knew, she was lying on a bed, her pants and panties down to her ankles, and someone was inside her, penetrating her. She at one point muttered, "Stop," but the perpetrator didn't stop. She could never get a good look at him, in part because she was fazing in and out, and also because the rapist was partially covering her face with parts of his powerful forearm and one of his large hands, obstructing her view. And then she remembered another one of her "Please stop" pleas was followed by a powerful blow to her left jaw, knocking her out.

Sanders pulled into the driveway of his home, a two-story, beige stucco house with a Spanish red-tile roof, brown trim, and crushed gray rocks lining the front and back yards. He was tired. His wife of two years, Lisa, would ask him, "How did the case go?" to which he would reply with one word: "Bad." He would skip dinner, preferring instead the company of two Heineken beers while he lay in bed flipping TV channels.

CHAPTER THREE

"Sorry I'm running a bit late, gang. Long lines at Maria's Bakery. Plus there was a truck accident on I-10."

It was a Monday morning at the Fort Bliss Trial Defense Services (TDS) office, and Sanders was five minutes late for the 9:00 a.m. weekly office staff meeting. He started opening bags and spreading out bagels, muffins, and doughnuts on the conference table.

Fort Bliss's TDS office consisted of five JAG attorneys and one paralegal. Captain Mike Clark, the senior defense counsel, led the meeting.

"Okay folks, a good Monday army morning to everyone," he said. "Mark, thanks for the goodies. My turn to buy next week." He grabbed a bran muffin and took a quick bite. "Just two things to cover, gang: cases I need to assign, and then the final plan for our office field trip this Friday. Now, as far as cases go, we just picked up a basic allowance for housing (BAH) fraud case out of Third Brigade. Mark, you already have an identical case from the same unit, which conflicts you out because of certain witnesses. Joe, I'm assigning you as lead defense counsel, and I'll tag team with you on this one as the second chair cocounsel."

"Sounds like a plan, boss," said Joe Ryan, a JAG reserve officer recently called up on active duty for a year. He was sipping from a coffee mug that read: "TDS—Defending Those Who Defend America."

"Next, we've got a child porn case out of the Sustainment Support Brigade."

"Oh, yuk," said Captain Linh Nguyen, a petite Vietnamese American out of Southern California and the only female on the TDS team.

"Well, Linh, I was actually thinking of assigning you and Jacob on this one."

"That'll work," Jacob Epstein said, chiming in. "I've got another child porn case. Got us a great computer forensics expert, Eric Hudson, out of Kansas City. Definitely a must to have a computer forensics expert for these kiddie porn cases." Jacob and Linh high-fived each other.

"All righty, then," Clark said. "And one last case to assign. A sexual assault case from one of the training units. Student soldiers straight out of basic training crashed out at some El Paso hotel over the weekend because it was the first weekend they were on pass status. There was too much fun going on—y'all know the deal: booze and dancing and sex. A classic date rape, she-said, he-said case. Mark, why don't you and Jacob team up on this one? It'll be a much easier case than that rape case you guys had Friday."

"Okay," Mark said, to which Jacob replied, "Roger."

"That's it for new cases, gang. Next, let's vote on our office field trip. Two options: visit White Sands in

New Mexico or hike one of the trails of the Franklin Mountains."

"White Sands blows," Jacob said. "Just a bunch of white sand. Looks like one big cocaine dump from one of the Juarez cartels."

Linh laughed out loud and smiled as she looked at Jacob.

"Well, that's your opinion, Jacob," Clark said. "Let's have a show of hands. Who's for visiting White Sands?"

Clark and Joe Ryan raised their hands. Clark then asked, "Who's for climbing the Franklin Mountains?"

Four hands went up: Mark's, Jacob's, Linh's, and Specialist Taylor's. Specialist Tom Taylor was the TDS paralegal.

"Well, democracy rules the day, I guess," Clark said. "Franklin Mountains it is. We'll take off from here at 10:00 a.m. this Friday."

CHAPTER FOUR

"So, how you holding up, Sergeant Adams?"

"Sir, get me outta here. I didn't rape Sonia."

It was Friday morning, exactly one week after the court-martial. Adams, already at the US Disciplinary Barracks prison at Fort Leavenworth, Kansas, was on the phone with his lead JAG attorney, Sanders. Normally, it would take around two weeks—maybe three—for a JAG defense lawyer to converse on the phone with his or her client, but Sanders had great rapport with a sergeant at the prison, one Sergeant Jamie Holmes, who knew how to effectively cut through the prison bureaucracy and make an inmate available for phone calls with his lawyer.

"I know, Sergeant," replied Sanders. "I'll do everything I can for you with the clemency packet. After that, you'll be assigned a JAG defense appellate lawyer who'll work your appeal."

"Roger, sir."

"Now, remember what we talked about right after the court-martial: keep your nose clean, stay busy—prison will assign you work duties—and we'll put the best clemency packet we can before Major General Wolfe, Fort Bliss's commanding general."

"Roger, sir."

"Work on your letter to Major General Wolfe. I'm gathering letters from your noncommissioned officers who support you."

"Appreciate that, sir."

"Thus far, I've only received a letter from Sergeant Ruiz. Sergeants Richardson and Buchanan said they wouldn't submit letters because the court-martial found you guilty."

"Figures."

"I still have to reach out to Sergeants Gonzalez and Dillard."

"They'll probably be a no-go too, sir."

"We'll try anyway. Never know. Now, what about family and relatives? I know we couldn't find them for the sentencing portion of your trial, but we can try again for clemency. Now, you haven't had contact with your mom for how long?"

"For all I know, she's dead, sir. Last I heard, she was in Vegas. Always a druggie."

"And your sister?"

"Dunno. Last I heard, she was in Philly. I haven't heard from her in ... oh ... two years or so."

"And your dad?"

"Same. Dunno. I think he's been in the Phoenix area for some time."

"Okay, I'll work on it."

"Thanks, sir. Get me outta here. I didn't rape Sonia."

CHAPTER FIVE

"Wow, this is great," Clark said. "Great scenery."

The five TDS lawyers and Specialist Taylor were atop El Paso's Franklin Mountains. It was a sunny, cloudless day, and the temperature was in the high nineties. A steady breeze at their elevation made it ten degrees cooler.

The TDS members would walk the trails of the Franklin Mountains that afternoon, and then the game plan was for everyone to meet up at Fort Bliss's German Club for beers.

Sanders was glad to have the day off, and he was enjoying the climbing, trail walking, and most of all, the scenery. But his thoughts often turned to the telephone conversation he'd had two hours prior. *"Get me outta here. I didn't rape Sonia."* The Adams case seemed to always be on his mind, reliving itself.

He followed the others heading down a narrow, curvy trail. The cool breeze felt good on his face.

Frigging clemency matters, he thought as he made his way down the trail. *We never get shit on those. Debatable if the juice is worth the squeeze on those packets; so much effort for so little outcome.*

CHAPTER SIX

"Don't tell me you're a True Believer on this one."

"I am."

"C'mon, Mark. Grow a brain, buddy."

"Jacob, hear me out."

The two were at Fort Bliss's German Club nursing their beers; the other TDS members had left already, concluding the end of the partial day-off office field trip.

A popular watering hole, the German Club was run by Germans. In fact, the German air force and German army had a significant footprint on Fort Bliss, because West Texas and parts of New Mexico had something Germany did not, at least not in ample supply: immense tracts of land to test missiles and air defense systems. Other allied nations also did such testing at Fort Bliss, but no other foreign ally had a significant presence like the Germans, who had their own school at the base and their own club open to the public.

"We've both had a lot of sexual assault cases, Jacob. Sergeant Adams just acts differently than past clients of mine."

"Oh, Mark, c'mon now. Don't give me the touchy-feely psychological rabble-babble. It's all about the evidence.

Follow the facts; have faith in the facts. Something like 80 percent of sexual assault victims know the perpetrator. In this case, it was the boyfriend-girlfriend thing. A big party for his birthday, with booze and drugs and lots of people hooking up, looking to score. She broke up with him that evening. He was pissed—his girlfriend breaks up with him on his birthday. She stayed at the party. And we know she flirted with other guys that night. She got drunk with her girlfriends who were also at the party. Later in the evening, our client took advantage of her. Oh, and did I mention DNA? Frigging DNA, Mark. It's conclusive. He raped her. Broke her jaw so bad she was on a liquid Jell-O diet for like three months. Dude, it's a solid case."

Sanders liked Jacob for a lot of reasons: he was smart and fun to work with, and Jacob Epstein was generally considered to be the best attorney in the TDS office. And Sanders liked and appreciated Jacob's direct, matter-of-fact approach to legal issues. Importantly, Sanders also knew Epstein was planning to leave the JAG Corps next year after the end of his three-year contractual obligation. He also knew Jacob and Linh were dating and planning on getting married, the game plan being that the young couple would move to Austin and set up a small criminal defense law firm. All this meant Epstein was on his way out—he didn't play games, and he didn't care about the rating chain and the all-important annual officer evaluation report. Jacob Epstein called them like he saw them.

Sanders took a sip of his beer, and then he said, "Jacob, hear me out—two things."

"It's a solid case, Mark."

"Just hear me out. One, Adams has maintained his innocence throughout the entire case. Even now, he maintains his innocence. He turned down a guilty plea of ten years—plead guilty to rape and you can't get more than ten years in the slammer, but he turned that down."

"I'm well aware of the deal the government offered us, Mark."

"And two, we didn't get the DNA expert we desired and requested. A proven and true DNA expert would have cost us like eight grand. Government fought our request and persuaded Judge Cohen at our motions hearing to rule that Dr. Ford, some part-time chemistry professor at a small college—the name of which I forget—was sufficient for the defense team."

"It's DNA, Mark."

"Yeah, well, we should have gotten Dr. Robertson from Fordham University. Yeah, his fee was high, but we would have gotten a real expert."

"Wouldn't have made a difference, Mark. Martinez was a true victim. She went to the hospital ASAP. Proper swaps. Rape kit. Eventually, the DNA matched. Our client's DNA."

"I'm not so sure, Jacob. She had sex that night with someone else after she and Adams had their 'one last time' sex. Dr. Ford didn't do a good job articulating a mixed-sample DNA."

"That's true."

"And there's no way Adams would have survived providency for a guilty plea."

"That's true too," said Epstein. He quickly sipped from his beer and said, "I frigging hate providency. That's a problem with the military criminal justice system. A guilty plea takes forever, like five hours, whereas in the civilian criminal justice system, a guilty plea takes some twenty minutes. A defendant having to explain what he did, that he did the crime, that he knew what he did was a crime, how he did the crime, step-by-step—hell, many defendants simply don't want to admit to such things. Plus, as you know, Mark, quite a few of our clients won't admit to criminal misconduct."

"Agreed."

"Bottom line, Mark, buddy, you're thinking about this case way too much. Our client raped his girlfriend—his ex-girlfriend. DNA is DNA, and he had motive too—he was pissed she was flirting with other dudes at the party; she had sex with someone else the very night of his birthday party, the very night she broke it off with him. Having Dr. Robertson on the defense team wouldn't have changed anything."

CHAPTER SEVEN

"Nice views, huh, babe?"

"Yes, it's beautiful," Lisa said. "Want another glass of wine, honey?"

"Yeah. Sure thing."

Mark and Lisa were on the second-story porch-deck of their home, enjoying the sunset's effect on the rocky edges of the Franklin Mountains. It was a Saturday evening, and the young couple had finished a late meal. Mark had worked all day at the office catching up on his cases. It had been a productive day, and now, after a long day of work on a Saturday, he was kicking back with his wife, enjoying a bottle of merlot.

"Here you go, Mark," Lisa said as she poured him another glass.

"Thanks, babe." They touched glasses.

Sitting in a comfortable lawn chair, Sanders thought about his current case load. The good news was he wasn't taking on more cases and clients. The bad news was that the reason he wasn't taking on more clients was because he was deploying—two months from now—to Iraq.

In that sense, it wasn't really bad news; he had, after all, volunteered for the combat-tour assignment because deployments were good for one's military career, and given that he was up for a promotion from captain to major in two years, a one-year deployment could only help his career progression. Of course, the bad part about the upcoming one-year deployment was it meant he would be separated from Lisa, but Lisa was supportive. She had her circle of friends in El Paso, namely military spouses such as herself, and Lisa was working on her yoga instructor certification, something she loved and spent a fair amount of time on. Lisa would keep herself busy during Mark's one-year absence; she would be okay.

Sanders took a sip of wine and concentrated on the beautiful Franklin Mountains. *Purple mountains*, he thought. *From the song "America the Beautiful."* It was beautiful, all right, that purple hue effect from the fading sunset, something the New Hampshire native had not seen until military orders brought him to America's Southwest.

"Honey, I'm going inside," Lisa said. "I'll start on the dishes. Join me?"

"In a minute, babe."

Lisa kissed him on his left cheek and entered the house through the deck door. Sanders, still sitting in his outdoor lawn chair, took another sip of wine, and then he thought, *DNA is DNA.* That's what Jacob had told him yesterday over beers at the German Club. *Dr. Robertson wouldn't have changed anything.*

Sanders began reliving key portions of Adams's trial, reassessing key facts and evidence.

Man, I am a True Believer with this case. He suddenly started reflecting back to the first time he had heard the term and its meaning.

"For you defense-oriented students, you defense-friendly types, y'all are True Believers." That's what the JAG criminal law professor had told Sanders's class, a class of some sixty JAG Officer Basic Course students at the Army JAG School in Charlottesville, Virginia. That was some six years ago. "Y'all believe your client when he tells you he didn't do it, that he's innocent. Me, I'm on the other side: Government Hack. I'd rather be a prosecutor any day than be a defense lawyer. Law and order. Criminals commit crimes, and unfortunately, the army does have some criminals in its ranks. Of course, every case has to be judged by its facts, by the evidence. And every defendant deserves a zealous defense and his day in court. I do believe in the system," the professor had said, "but I tend not to believe the criminally accused. I'm a Government Hack prosecutor, not a True Believer defense counsel. If it's United States versus Sergeant John Doe, I'm with the good old US of A."

Sanders took another sip of wine. *True Believer,* he thought. *We didn't have the best DNA expert; Sergeant Adams maintained his innocence throughout; Sergeant Adams is believable.*

"Fuck it," he said out loud. He took a gulp of wine, finishing his glass. *I've got an idea.*

CHAPTER EIGHT

"Do you have a photo of him?"

"Yes, Mr. Jaworski." Sanders handed Jaworski an enlarged color version of Sergeant Adams's enlisted record brief (ERB), a one-page document outlining Adams's military career to include assignments, test scores, and educational background. In the bottom right-hand corner of the ERB was a full-frontal photo of Sergeant Adams in his class A uniform, complete with military ribbons.

"Well, it's not the best photo quality, but it will do," said Jaworski. He ran his fingers over the page, and then he brought it close to his eyes. He started concentrating.

Robert Jaworski, age sixty-three, was a psychic based out of Las Cruces, New Mexico, some twenty-five miles north of El Paso. His home was a small white-brick rambler with a short asphalt driveway. He took clients over the phone and in person. He also took part in El Paso's popular quarterly Psychic Fair.

It was at one of El Paso's Psychic Fairs about a year ago that Mark and Lisa had first met Jaworski. Mark had seen an ad advertising the fair in the *El Paso Times* and thought it might be a fun way to spend a Saturday afternoon. When he and Lisa arrived at the hotel conference room where the fair was held, they immediately noticed more people were lined up to have sessions with Jaworski than the other psychics. They signed their names on a clipboard log and got their readings.

Jaworksi was a native El Pasoan. Growing up, he enjoyed playing outdoors with his friends; football and baseball were his favorite sports. He also enjoyed climbing the Franklin Mountains, and he devoted a fair amount of his spare time to his stamp collection. He was a good student, solid in most subjects, and above average in math. But his young life would take a significant turn on his fourteenth birthday.

It was a cloudless, hot summer day, and Jaworski was in the front passenger seat of his father's 1956 Chevy. His dad, a successful small businessman and real estate investor, was behind the wheel, taking his son out to their favorite ice cream parlor as part of the birthday festivities. Suddenly, out of nowhere, a huge truck swerved into the Jaworkskis' driving lane, instinctively causing Mr. Jaworski to swerve off the road in an attempt to avoid the inevitable collision. The result: their car avoided a massive collision but instead rolled over four times.

Numerous broken bones were the injuries of the elder Jaworski, while the teenaged Jaworski ended up in a coma that lasted exactly two weeks. Headaches ensued shortly after the teenager "woke up" from his comatose state—headaches followed by visions, with the former eventually fading, but the later growing in both frequency and intensity as Jaworski aged. At eighteen, Jaworksi entered college at St. Mary's University in San Antonio, and in his spare time, he began to read everything he could about clairvoyants, psychic phenomena, numerology, and the paranormal in an attempt to gain an understanding of the visions he experienced in his mind. He also started giving readings to fellow college students, charging five dollars for thirty minutes of his time. Business was brisk.

Upon graduating from college, Jaworski embarked on a successful career as a coffee broker, an occupation that brought him to numerous cities in North America and faraway lands in Europe, Africa, and parts of Asia. Ten years ago, Jaworski retired in Las Cruces, his hobby of providing psychic readings alive and well, just like in his college years. His clients included the FBI and a few police departments for assistance with unsolved cases. Then there was El Paso's quarterly Psychic Fair, which was also good for business. But undoubtedly, Jaworski's big moneymaker was providing readings to some big-shot Hollywood actor/producer who was fanatic about not letting anyone or the media know he was getting psychic readings. This big-money client would meet with Jaworski five times a year in Vegas, paying the psychic five grand per visit, plus travel and lodging. Jaworski, loyal to the core, was tight-lipped and never revealed this famous client of his.

"And what about the victim?" Jaworski said in his soft voice. "Do you have a photo of her?"

"Yes, I do, sir," Sanders said. "Four, in fact." He reached in his book bag and pulled out a folder containing the four photos. He opened the manila folder and handed the photos to Jaworski.

"Hmmm? Yes. Well, let's see," Jaworski said. He closed his eyes. Sanders, uncomfortable starring at

Jaworski, started scanning the room, a small office space within Jaworski's house. Two windows faced east, and the blinds were down. Every wall was dark green, and only a tiny bed lamp lit the room, its light-yellow bulb illuminating the room with a similar hue. Sanders also noticed a small wooden bookshelf to his right, its contents hardcover books all about spirituality. Separating him and Jaworski was a tiny round table completely covered with a purple tablecloth. A deck of tarot cards sat to Sanders's left. Four photos of Sonia Martinez and Adams's ERB occupied the center of the table. The small room's floor was covered with a light-green shag carpet, a throwback to the seventies.

Jaworski held up Adams's ERB and one of Martinez's photos up to his eyes.

"So your question is, did this soldier rape this girl? Is that right, Mark?"

"Yes, that's right, Mr. Jaworski."

Jaworski placed the photo and the ERB page back on the table. He rubbed his eyes with both hands. Jaworski was wearing his trademark white three-piece suit and a Panama fedora; the latter he wore whether he was indoors or outdoors.

"Yes, this girl was raped," Jaworski said. "I see there was a big party, but it was not a gang rape. She was raped in a small side room of a home. A small bedroom. Only her and the rapist. There were lots of people, but they were mostly outside, partying. I see kegs of beer. A large punch bowl too."

"And?" Sanders asked. "Was it Sergeant Adams who raped her, sir?"

"No," Jaworski said. "No, he didn't. He's not an angel, this Sergeant Adams. He's engaged in, shall we say, 'questionable activities,' but he didn't rape her."

"Do you see the rapist, Mr. Jaworski? And if you do, can you describe him? Can you tell me who he is?"

"He's someone who looks similar to Sergeant Adams."

CHAPTER NINE

"Thanks for seeing me on short notice, Jacob."

"Sure, no problem. Anytime."

Sanders and Epstein were at Fort Bliss's German Club. It was a Tuesday night after work, and the two army criminal defense lawyers were in their duty uniforms, the ACU, the army combat uniform. Mark said, "Two Coronas, please," as a waitress walked by their table.

"So, what's up?" Jacob asked. "I'm guessing this is about the Adams case."

"Bingo, buddy. Correct as usual. I need some help, some assistance."

"Okay."

"I need a private investigator to look into the Adams case. Don't you know one out of Houston?"

"Actually, I know a few private investigators. One in Houston and a couple out of Dallas."

"Didn't you use the Houston guy for a court-martial at Fort Hood?"

"Actually, that was Captain Jeffrey Watkins's case. I was second chair. Jeffrey discovered the services of one Dale Owens. He's the PI out of Houston. Good results, actually—found a former boyfriend of the alleged victim of a sexual assault case. Turned the case around for us."

The waitress arrived with the two beers, and Sanders handed her a ten-dollar bill. He then said, "Jacob, I need Mr. Owens's contact information."

"He doesn't come cheap, you know."

"I don't care."

"Our client's parents actually paid for Owens's services in that court-martial. I think it came out to five grand or something."

"I don't care, Jacob."

"Man, you really are a True Believer on this one, huh?"

"Yep. I'm all in, buddy. Yesterday, I hired Dr. Robertson to look over the DNA portion of the case file."

"No way."

"Way."

"Man, how much did that run you?"

"Four grand. He gave me a discount. He's got an office in New York City and another one in Cleveland. He told me to FedEx the pertinent portion of the case file to his Cleveland office and that it might take him like two months to give me his findings."

"Why two months?"

"He's on sabbatical right now in Leipzig, Germany. All my communications with Dr. Robertson have been through e-mail."

Jacob took a sip from his beer.

"Four grand, huh? How'd you pay for that?"

"Credit card."

"Does Lisa know?"

"Not yet."

"Why do you need a private investigator?"

"Jacob, we counted twenty-one people at that party. I'm going through my witness list again, calling them all back, going over their stories, making sure I didn't miss anything."

"We didn't miss anything, Mark."

"I'm not so sure, Jacob. And I want to be sure."

"So, do you plan on using Owens to interview the party attendees or what?"

"Maybe. Some of them have moved on—you know, people who get new jobs and move to other locales. I'm sure I'll have some difficulty locating all the witnesses to include soldiers who are now stationed elsewhere. Plus, I'm having trouble locating Adams's sister, father, and mother. Maybe the private investigator can help me track these people down."

"All right, buddy. I've got Owens's business card in my office. I know he's got a website too. Dale Owens, Houston, Texas. I'm sure if you Google him, you'll get him."

"Thanks, Jacob. By the way, how's Linh?"

"Great."

"Still planning on getting out of the JAG Corps and moving to Austin?"

"Yep. Linh's game too."

"Cool."

"Yeah, she's a great gal. My parents are so-so with it—you know, the Jewish thing; they'd prefer I'd hook up with a Jewish girl. But they'll turn around over time. I'll tell you, my parents were very excited and approving of Linh's education—Stanford undergrad and University of Michigan Law School."

"Nice."

Jacob took a quick sip of beer, and then he changed the subject. "Your deployment is in less than two months, huh?"

"Yeah. I'm actually looking forward to it," Mark said. "It's a good career move; I just want to get there and get it over with."

"Great," Jacob said, and then he stood up. "Hey, thanks for the beer, Mark. I gotta go. Meeting Linh at eight."

CHAPTER TEN

"So you don't remember seeing anyone who resembled Keyshawn?"

"Uh … nope," said Paco Salinas.

"Thank you, Mr. Salinas. Please feel free to call me or e-mail me, should you know of anything that might help me with Keyshawn's case."

"Sure thing."

Click.

It was a Thursday night, and Sanders was at the TDS office going over his list of all the attendees at the party the night Martinez was brutally raped. It was seven o'clock, and he had just a few more calls to make.

He took a sip of coffee and looked at his e-mails on the computer monitor screen. There were three unanswered e-mails; he read the subject lines:

"Blood Drive at Beaumont Hospital." He deleted that one and clicked on the second e-mail.

"CLE on Environment Law in Albuquerque."

He deleted that one too and then read the subject line of the third e-mail.

"When you coming home? Friend needs job-hunting tips for federal government job."

It was Lisa. He double-clicked the e-mail.

Mark,

When are you coming home? Let me know if it's gonna be another late night. If so, I'll place your dinner in the refrigerator and you can microwave it later. Also, my friend Susan called me tonight. You remember Susan from Colorado State? Well, she's thinking about applying for jobs with the federal government, but she tells me the process is overwhelming for her right now. Any resume tips? Any tips at all?

Love, Lisa

He hit the reply button.

Babe,

It's another late night, so keep my dinner in the fridge. As for Susan, I do remember her, and all I can say is for her to get on the USAJOBS website, the website for federal government jobs. She's probably already doing this, but there are other websites that are a waste of time. I've heard it's really tough to break in with the federal government.

One tip is to make sure her resume has the same words outlined in the particular job announcement. Also, tell her to start small, GS-7 or something. Easier to get those lower-level entry jobs. Once she's in the federal government service, she's in. Great job security, and promotions can be fast, which is why I recommend she start with lower-ranking jobs.

I've also heard a good way to break into the system is simply to volunteer somewhere with the government and then show interest in a particular position. Volunteering apparently works. I know a couple of folks who got jobs that way. These government employees— some of them work in JAG offices—told me applying online can sometimes be a waste of time, because the agency gets all these applications, but they often already know who they're going to give the job to even before the job opening is announced; in essence, the job announcement is just an appearance to protect the agency and to make them look fair. Networking is key too; it's who you know that counts. I recommend Susan volunteer with an agency she would like to work for. She should volunteer for like three months and then express interest in a job opening with that agency.

Hope this helps.

Love you,
Mark

He hit the send button, and then he took a sip of coffee. He looked at his list of people to track down:

Clyde Webber—was at party. Whereabouts unknown; no hits.

Angel Montgomery—was at party. Whereabouts unknown; no hits.

Carol Adams—mother. Vegas? No phone numbers found.

Marcia Adams—sister, Philadelphia area.

Ronald Adams—father, Phoenix area.

He dialed Montgomery's phone number. After one ring he heard, "This number is no longer in service."

He crossed out Ms. Montgomery's name, and then he dialed the phone number he had for Marcia Adams.

Earlier in the day, he had done basic computer searches for any Marcia Adams in the Philadelphia area. He had done the same for Keyshawn's father, Ronald Adams, looking up that name for any hits around Phoenix. There was one hit for a Marcia Adams in Bensalem, Pennsylvania, and no hits for a Ronald Adams in Phoenix, though there was a Ronald Adams in Flagstaff.

He dialed the Bensalem number, and after five rings, a voice answered with, "Hi, you've reached Marcia. I'm not in right now. Please leave a message."

"Ms. Adams, my name is Captain Mark Sanders. I'm a lawyer with the Army JAG Corps, and I represented your brother at his recent court-martial. I'd like to ask you a few questions. Please call me at your earliest convenience. I can be reached at …" and he gave her his office, home, and cell phone number. He then dialed the Flagstaff number, and after speaking to a Mr. Ronald Adams for some five minutes, he knew he had the wrong Ronald Adams.

CHAPTER ELEVEN

"Sergeant Adams, this is Captain Sanders. How you holding up?"

"Doing the best I can, sir, but prison sucks."

It was a Friday afternoon, and Sanders had just received notice from the JAG prosecution team that Major General Wolfe, Commander, Fort Bliss, had rejected Adams's clemency request.

"Well, Sergeant, the purpose of my call is to see how things are going and also to inform you Major General Wolfe—like we expected—didn't give us anything on clemency."

"Figures," Adams said.

There was an awkward silence.

"Sergeant Adams, our case will automatically go on appeal. You'll be assigned a JAG appellate lawyer."

"Roger, sir."

"It can take two years or so before a case is heard by the appellate court."

Silence.

"I'll be deploying soon to Iraq, but I'm gonna keep in touch with you, Sergeant Adams."

"Appreciate it, sir."

"I'm still working things on my end, Sergeant."

"Okay," said Adams, "but I didn't do it, sir." He was sitting on a metal chair in a closed room. Sanders had earlier told him the government wasn't supposed to listen in on communications between inmates and their attorneys, but Adams trusted no one and kept his talking crisp and simple.

CHAPTER TWELVE

"I need three grand up front. As things progress, I'll let you know the fees for other necessary services."

"What do I get for the three grand?" Sanders asked Dale Owens. The two were at a Starbucks in the rapidly expanding northeast section of El Paso. It was a Friday night, three days since Sanders had asked Epstein for Owens's contact information. It so happened that one of Owens's cases was in nearby Las Cruces, New Mexico. The two agreed to meet in El Paso to discuss the work ahead in the Adams case.

"Initial computer searches, more than your basic Google stuff," Owens said. "For three grand, I do searches of certain databases. Marcia Adams and Ronald Adams, right?"

"Yes," replied Sanders. "Those are the persons I'm searching for, the sister and father of my client. Also Carol Adams, my client's mother, and also Clyde Webber and Angel Montgomery."

"Okay," replied Owens, typing the names into his laptop. He was tall and broad-shouldered, and he wore designer jeans and a blue long-sleeve polo shirt. Sanders thought, *He looks like Charles Barkley.*

"The mother, her last known residence was Vegas?"

"Yes, at least that's what Sergeant Adams told me."

"And Sergeant Adams, his first name?"

"Keyshawn."

"Age?"

"Twenty-five."

"Sister's age?"

"I think she's twenty-two. I did find a Marcia Adams in Bensalem, Pennsylvania; left a message."

"Good," said Owens. "And the father's age?"

"I think forty-four."

"Good—about my age. I'm forty-five."

"How is that good?"

"If and when I find him, maybe we have things in common. I've worked some cases in Phoenix; got some good contacts there. Hopefully, that's where he's at."

Sanders sipped from his cappuccino. "So three grand gets the ball rolling, huh?"

"Correct," Owens said. "Here's my business card."

"Thanks."

"You can call me anytime, office or cell. My principal means of communication is e-mail. I send you updates."

Sanders nodded in approval, and then he said, "Do you accept credit cards, Mr. Owens?"

CHAPTER THIRTEEN

"You did what?"

"Babe, let me explain."

"Mark, how could you? We're stretched financially as it is. I'm not working right now, and we've got the Alaskan cruise coming up. Four grand for DNA analysis, three grand to a private investigator. Money doesn't grow on trees, you know."

"I know, babe, but it's money well spent."

The young couple was at their favorite restaurant, Cattleman's, a renowned steakhouse about forty-five minutes east of El Paso that was featured on the Travel Channel. Mark was working on his rib eye, while Lisa was enjoying a filet mignon. A bottle of malbec was their wine selection.

"That's seven grand, Mark. And you're telling me the private investigator will cost more down the road as he does more work. How in God's name do you plan on paying for this? You still owe on your student loans, you know, and we have a big mortgage."

"Honey, I know all that. I've figured it out. My upcoming deployment to Iraq will give us almost an extra two thousand dollars per month, and it's tax-free. Combat pay, family separation pay, all that stuff."

"I hope you know what you're doing, Mark."

"I do, babe."

One Month Later

CHAPTER FOURTEEN

"You're all in, huh?"

"Yep, chips are in the pot. I feel like things are not in my control; it's up to Dr. Robertson and Mr. Owens at this point."

Mark and Jacob were drinking beer at State Line Barbecue, a popular restaurant straddling the Texas–New Mexico border. It was a Thursday night, and the two had decided to get together one last time before Mark's deployment to Iraq.

"I admire your resolve, Mark. You're spending a lot of money on the Adams case, but I don't think it'll change anything."

"We'll see," Mark said. "I'm just doing my best, advocating for a client." He looked at the beer selection menu and then said, "So, how's Linh?"

"Great. She's an awesome gal."

"And how's the house?" Jacob had bought a house in El Paso's west side, just like Mark and Lisa had.

"Oh, frankly, it's a mixed bag. Nice to own a home, but it doesn't come cheap. Property taxes are a killer here in El Paso. You know why, right? Why the property taxes are so high here?"

"Well, Texas doesn't have state income tax, so I guess they have to make up for the revenues somewhere."

"That's part of it, Mark, but that's not the real cause. Nope, the real reason why property taxes are atrocious here is because so many of the students in El Paso are actually from Juarez. What pays for all these schools in El Paso? Property taxes, of course. Good old American taxpayers picking up the tab once again. Many El Paso residents have relatives in Juarez. Juarez students come here to live with uncle and/or auntie during the week to get their free American education. El Paso schools can't check or verify students' true residency on account of some court cases. A buddy of mine told me traffic at the border port of entry is incredible on Monday mornings because that's when the Juarez students come in to live with relatives and attend school for the week. Traffic is equally incredible on Fridays, because that's when they return to Juarez to be with their families."

"I didn't know that," Mark said. "I always wondered why there were a lot of schools in El Paso."

Suddenly, a waitress passed by him, and he ordered two Coronas.

"So you'll be leaving the JAG Corps in about six months, huh?"

"Yeah," Jacob said. "I've enjoyed the JAG; I really have. But I won't miss the morning physical fitness stuff, the height and weight requirements, and all the nonsense bureaucracy. The army is so inefficient. So much online training, tons of surveys, and then that stupid Defense Travel System, DTS."

"Yeah, I hate DTS too," Mark said. "When we have a court-martial at Fort Hood, it's such a chore to use DTS to plan our trip—flight, hotel, car rental. You know the running joke right, what DTS stands for?"

"I think I heard it once, but I forgot. Refresh my memory, buddy."

"DTS stands for the Do Not Travel System."

Sanders chuckled and said, "True. They make it so hard to travel, man."

"Yeah, the system is broken, Mark. There's so much paperwork with DTS: cost-comparison sheets, scanning and uploading receipts to get reimbursed. What a mess. The government makes it so hard just to do something as simple as travel."

"Agreed," Mark said.

The waitress arrived with the two Coronas, and she then took Mark and Jacob's orders; both ordered the brisket special.

The two touched glasses. "Cheers," Jacob said.

"Cheers," Mark said.

"And there's so much onus on the service member," Jacob said. "For example, we have to check our own files for upcoming boards. How many awards do you have? Is all the paperwork in place? The personnel section should do all that for us. There's a lot of room for improvement, lemme tell ya. Anyway, did you hear the latest?"

"Latest on what?"

"Latest news about the hot topic in the army Jag Corps?"

"Nah, what's the latest?"

"Some film crew is doing some movie about sexual assaults in the military. I think the movie will be entitled *The Silent War* or some shit like that. Not sure who is behind the movie—probably some think-tank/advocacy group type of outfit."

"I didn't hear anything about that."

"Oh, yeah," Jacob said as he took a quick sip of beer. "I heard this from Carl Jennings, who's stationed in the DC area. Remember Carl?"

"Yeah, great guy. West Pointer. Went to law school at William and Mary. Funny dude too."

"Yeah, well, Carl told me apparently the film's producer is picking real cases out of the military branches, five cases in all because there's a Coast Guard case. So the film will interview five sexual assault victims from each branch."

"Well, I hope the movie gets it right," Mark said. "The military in many ways is like society at large. We do have sexual assaults and rapes in the military, but so does society at large. I'm not convinced we have more of a problem than what takes place on many college campuses. Many sexual assault cases are quite defendable at court-martial."

"I concur, counsel," Jacob said. "Well articulated. They need to pick the correct five cases to show what's really going on; it's actually a complex topic, you know. Most purported sexual assault victims know their assailant. It's the date rape thing; pretty complicated stuff."

Ten minutes later, the waitress, a tall, young Latina with long black hair, arrived with the barbecue brisket.

"Here you go, guys," she said as she placed the hot plates before the patrons.

Mark said, "Can I have some more water, please? And we'll have another round of Coronas."

"Sure," replied the waitress.

Mark and Jacob starting eating, and the conversation soon shifted to the immense amount of construction occurring on Fort Bliss on account of the First Armored Division moving from Germany to El Paso. Suddenly, Mark said, "Think we made the right decision to go panel jury for the Adams case?"

"Yeah, we did. Colonel Cohen might have given a tougher sentence," Jacob said. "Like many military judges, he's a Government Hack."

CHAPTER FIFTEEN

"Wow. Mark, Mark, see it? The whale?"

"Yeah, babe, I see it."

"This is awesome. Beautiful. Gorgeous."

Mark and Lisa were on the second-floor deck of a huge cruise ship. It was gray and misty out, but the young couple could clearly see a whale in the small nearby bay. Lisa started taking photos. "This is the best trip ever, Mark."

"You bet, babe."

A JAG friend of Mark's, Brian Eaton, a fellow JAG officer stationed at Fort Lewis, Washington, near Seattle, had spoken favorably about Alaskan cruises, and Mark figured such a cruise would be a great vacation prior to his Iraqi deployment. Green and mountainous Alaska, with its whales, grizzly bears, strong rivers, beautiful oceans and bays, melting glaciers—such a contrast to the upcoming hot desert climate that was awaiting him, the "sandbox called Iraq," as soldiers referred to it.

Lisa kept taking photos for the next ten minutes, while Mark kept taking in the gorgeous scenery.

CHAPTER SIXTEEN

"There it is, honey, I see it. That's my luggage."

Mark maneuvered around a few people at the El Paso Airport baggage claim area, and in a few seconds, Lisa's last luggage piece was in range, and Mark grabbed it by the handle. "There," he said as he pulled up the brown suitcase and placed it on a luggage trolley. His cell phone suddenly rang; he reached into the left inside interior pocket of his sports jacket.

"Hello, this is Mark Sanders."

"Mr. Sanders, I'm Marcia Phillips. You called me about a month ago and left a message."

Mark and Lisa started walking toward the exit to get to the long-term parking section. Sanders was pulling a large luggage piece with his left hand and holding his cell phone with his right one.

"I apologize, Ms. Phillips, but your name doesn't ring a bell with me. You said I called you some time ago?"

"Yes. I used to be Marcia Adams. I got married and moved."

"Oh, oh, yes, yes, Ms. Adams … uh, I mean, Ms. Phillips. Thanks. Thanks for getting back to me. Well, as you know from the message I left you, I was one of your brother's defense lawyers, and—"

"I know that," she said abruptly. "Well, I don't have much to say to you, Mr. Sanders. I haven't seen or heard from my brother in like, oh, two years or something like that."

Mark and Lisa walked through a set of glass doors that automatically opened. El Paso's hot, dry climate hit them right away.

"Yes, well, I understand that, Ms. Phillips. I've been trying to reach your mother as well and—"

"My mother died last year in Henderson, Nevada. Drug overdose."

"Oh, I'm sorry to hear that, ma'am."

There was an awkward silence.

"And I've been trying to reach your father as well. I've been told he's in the Phoenix area and—"

"I don't have any contact with my father, Mr. Sanders."

"Oh, I see."

Another awkward silence. Sanders was getting ready to say thank you and hang up, but he figured he'd probe just a bit.

"Uh, Ms. Phillips. Why is it that you don't have any contact with your father?"

Silence. Then he heard, "Because he raped me when I was fourteen."

CHAPTER SEVENTEEN

"Thank you," said Sanders as the flight attendant handed him a cup of coffee. He and close to two hundred soldiers, contractors, and government civilian employees were on a huge airliner, and their estimated arrival time to their destination, Kuwait International Airport, was fourteen hours away. Sanders had spent the past week training and preparing for his Iraqi deployment at an East Coast army base. The flight had taken off some fifteen minutes earlier, and Sanders was now drinking coffee and reading essays by George Orwell, including one particular essay entitled "Shooting an Elephant."

Sanders, occupying a window seat, looked outside the tiny circular window to his right. He saw thick, puffy white clouds below his elevation. For no particular reason, he started thinking randomly:

Iraq: *I hope it goes well.*
Lisa: *I hope she'll be all right.*
And the Adams case: *Adams's sister's revelation over the phone two weeks ago is huge, of course. I e-mailed PI Owens right away and told him to kill the search for the mom, since she's dead, and I told him to focus on the father, a rapist.*

Sanders sipped from his coffee cup, and he stared at the white, puffy clouds. *What the hell?* he thought. He took out a yellow legal notepad and a pen from his book bag, and he started writing notes:

> Just because the father raped his daughter doesn't mean the father is the rapist in the Adams case.
>
> Is the sister credible? Was she really raped, or is she making a false accusation?
>
> No word from Dr. Robertson yet. We know Adams and Sonia had sex that night. That hurts our case. What will Robertson get us?
>
> Will Owens find the father, Ronald Adams?

Lots of questions, he thought. *Lots of gaps.*

He decided to just write down whatever came to his mind.

Game plan was to do everything I could to raise doubts and somehow try to get a new trial.

Dr. Robertson: $4K

Owens: $3K + $2K for more Internet searches and travel expenses. $5K and counting.

What's important is not what you believe, but what you can prove. And what can I prove right now? Nothing—nothing yet. Not much I can do on my end; it's all up to Robertson and Owens, and the appellate lawyer.

Am I really a True Believer? Yes, in this case, I am. Overall, not really. TDS—man, I've seen and heard about some crazy shit. Before going to law school and joining the army JAG, I thought many of the Hollywood movies were make-believe; the world doesn't really work that way. Great childhood in rural New Hampshire, I must say, but you get out of that environment and learn rather quickly not everything is nice and bucolic and Republican-Libertarian New Hampshire.

Brian Eaton had a case at Fort Lewis involving a gang war shooting. Here at Fort Bliss, we had some crazy civilian husband of a female soldier who shot and killed his wife and then turned the gun on himself and blew his brains out. Joe McGraw, another JAG buddy, had a case out of Fort Hood where a female soldier gets done with morning physical training and then gets inside her car to drive back to her apartment to shower and then get ready to go to work. As she was driving, a man with a black face mask over his face suddenly popped up from the backseat and directed her to drive off to some isolated country road, where he raped her and placed a gun to her head. He almost killed her; the only thing saving her was she told the rapist, "I'm a mother. See, here's a picture of my little girl. Please don't kill me." She had the photo in her wallet.

A case like that is like straight out of Hollywood. There are bad people out there, and there are monsters out there. Ain't nothing wrong with Government Hacks—the world needs prosecutors. Ain't nothing wrong with True Believers, either. But not all defense lawyers are True Believers; they're just doing their job, defending their client as best they can.

Sanders took a sip of coffee.

True Believer—yes. I'm a True Believer in Adams's case, but maybe not in all my cases. A good test is one's reaction to John Grisham's great book and sole work of nonfiction, *The Innocent Man*. Dad's reaction when he read the book was just how unfortunate the whole case was, an innocent man on death row who, thanks to DNA, was rightfully exonerated. My reaction, and Mom's reaction, was quite different. Yes, we were of course glad that justice had been served and an innocent man was rightfully, over time, acquitted for a crime he had not committed. But that innocent man was not truly innocent, in my view and in Mom's opinion. Hell, two women had truthfully testified in court that the accused had sexually assaulted them in the past. I'm glad DNA proved he was innocent of a brutal murder, and I'm glad he was set free, but I can see how a jury convicted him. DNA in the 1980s was not what DNA is now or was in the late 1990s.

I hope DNA exonerates Adams, and I hope Owens can find the elder Adams.

CHAPTER EIGHTEEN

"All right, how 'bout 'em Padres sticking it to the Giants. Round of beer for everyone," Owens said for the half dozen or so bar patrons to hear. He looked to his right. "My man, what you drinking?"

"Sam Adams," said Ronald Adams.

"Sam Adams it is. Bartender, Sam Adams for me and the kind gentleman here. And whatever the other patrons want to drink. I'm buying this round. Padres just beat the Giants, and I made me five grand. Got me a good bookie in Vegas. All legal, of course."

Owens was finally able to track down Ronald Adams in Phoenix after some serious hustling. Pounding the pavement had produced some results, but ultimately, it came down to a great tip from a local cop who informed Owens the Phoenix Police Department was keeping a close eye on Adams, a car mechanic known to dabble in drug trafficking if the price was right.

The bartender brought the beers, and Owens immediately said, "Cheers," as he touched bottles with Adams. "Oh, and bartender, keep a running a tab, *por favor.*"

Owens had marveled at just how young Adams looked. Though forty-four, Adams looked like he was in his early thirties. And sitting next to Adams was a beautiful young Latina wearing tight faded jeans and a tight yellow tank top. She was nursing a margarita. *She can't be more than twenty-five*, Owens thought.

"Diamondbacks suck this year, and I think the Giants will make the playoffs, but my gut—and my bookie—told me to go with the Padres," Owens said loudly. "Always go with your gut, especially if your bookie agrees. What do you think, brother? Go with the gut, right?"

"Sounds good to me," replied Adams.

"And what are you drinking, dear senorita? Looks like a margarita to me."

"Yes, a margarita, and I guess I can have another one."

"Bartender, a margarita for the kind young lady."

"Name's Bob Foster," Owens said, lying. He shook hands with the Latina and with Adams.

"Cielo Ramirez," said the Latina. "Ron Adams," said Adams.

"Cool. Nice to meet you both. This is my third time in lovely Phoenix. I buy used cars from all over the Southwest. Then we disassemble them in El Paso—got me a huge junkyard out there—and we sell the auto parts in Juarez, Mexico. Good business—all legit, of course."

Adams said nothing.

"So, Ron, my brother, what type of work do you do?"

"Car mechanic. Work on trucks too."

"Cool. That's cool," responded Owens, although he'd already known the answer.

"You got a business card? I might need some work on my hauler truck someday."

"Sure. Name of the place is Doug's Garage." He reached for his wallet and peered inside. "Ah, shit, man. I'm out of business cards."

"No problem, brother. Doug's Garage. I'll Google it up; we cool." He sipped from his beer and switched topic. "Ever been to El Paso, Ron?"

"Uh, yeah. Yep. I've been there."

"City is growing fast. Lots of construction. Army's moving a division from Germany to Fort Bliss. I'm so blessed, man," Owens said, lying. "My son is in the army, and he's stationed at Bliss."

"Mine too," Adams said as he sipped some beer.

"You don't say? What a coincidence, man."

"Yep."

"So I got to ask you, when's the last time you've been to El Paso?"

"Oh, 'bout a year ago."

"Cool," said Owens. "Yeah, I'm real proud of my son. Army soldier. We just celebrated his twenty-fifth birthday. He's deploying to Iraq soon. Me and the ex-wife—she was a great mother, but a lousy wife, lemme tell ya. Anyway, we's still on good terms, and we decided to throw a big birthday party for our son before he deploys. How old's your son?"

"'Bout the same age as your son."

"Cool, man, coincidence there too. What unit is he in?"

"I don't know," Adams said. Then Owens immediately said, "Another beer, Ron?"

"I'm still working on this one, but I'll have another one. Sure."

"Bartender, two more Sam Adams."

"Okay," said the bartender, a heavyset middle-aged Hispanic man sporting a goatee and two gold earrings.

A few minutes later, the bartender brought the beer bottles, and that's when Owens said, "Folks, I'm heading to the outdoor patio where smoking is allowed. I want to celebrate some more, and nothing beats a good cigar, especially after winning some good money. Care to join me, brother?"

"Sure," said Adams. The Latina smiled.

Owens told the bartender, "Keep the tab running, amigo. We're heading outside to smoke." He got up and started walking toward the back end of the sports bar toward the outdoor patio. Adams and the Latina followed him, carrying their drinks. When he got to the patio, he noticed there were only two small tables that were unoccupied—one to the left and one toward a corner, at the far end of the patio. He decided to sit at the far end table.

Owens was dressed in faded jeans, and he sported an Arizona Diamondbacks jersey. He was wearing sunglasses too, but not dark sunglasses; he always preferred brown-red shaded sunglasses where people could still see his eyes. Everything thus far was going to plan. The local cop had provided some key information on Adams, information that Owens knew how to use to his advantage. For example, the cop had told him Adams liked sports, so Owens played that angle. The cop also said Adams was a mechanic and that he enjoyed an occasional cigar. Owens was playing that angle too.

Owens lit up a cigar for himself and then he handed cigars to Adams and the Latina. The trio was sitting at the small corner table. It was eight o'clock.

"La Libertad Robusto from the Dominican Republic," Owens said. "Fine cigar. About five dollars a pop. Here, lemme light yours, senorita." He flicked his lighter, and the Latina leaned forward toward him to get her cigar lit.

"And Ron, here you go." He reached over and handed his lighter to Adams so he could light up.

"Oh, this is the way to celebrate a five-grand win. Chalk up a *W*, a nice win. Sports betting, man—you win some and you lose some, but it's always fun to play. 'Course, winning's better than losing."

The Latina smiled. Owens glanced at Adams, who was enjoying his cigar.

Everything's going according to plan, Owens thought. *Stay focused. I just need him to go to the bathroom.*

Owens started drinking his beer fast.

"How's that margarita?" he asked the girl.

"Oh, fine, sir. Thank you."

"Call me Bob, please."

"Thank you, Bob."

"And Ron, another beer? What you say? You're not gonna be a lightweight on me now, right? Not on a night when I won me some good coin."

"Well, I'm still working on this one here."

"Oh, waitress," Owens said loudly. "Another round, please. I'm running a tab. Two Sam Adams and one margarita."

The trio continued drinking and smoking.

"Yeah, I don't know 'bout you, Ron, but I'm a lucky dude. Business is going real good. Great son and daughter—both my kids turned out great, both serving in the army. Ex-wife is a good mother. Our marriage fizzled, and then it sucked big time, and then we divorced, but we's on good terms." He blew cigar smoke in the air. "I'm gonna miss my son. Iraq, man. Hope that shit ends soon."

Adams said nothing.

The drinks arrived, and Owens proposed toasts.

"To the Padres, who made me five grand tonight."

"To the Padres," the trio said.

"To the good old US of A."

"To the good old US of A," they echoed.

"To the real estate bubble. May housing prices rebound."

"To the real estate bubble. May housing prices rebound."

"To our sons and daughters in the armed forces keeping us free."

"To our sons and daughters in the armed forces keeping us free."

Owens downed the rest of his beer. "Ron," he said, "are you driving tonight, or is senorita here driving? I propose we do one last round of drinks, and then we slow it down over coffee."

"Sounds like a plan," Adams said. He took a puff from his cigar. "But I have to hit the john first." He got up. "Excuse me. I'll be right back."

"Sure thing," Owens said. He waited until Adams was out of sight, and then he got up.

"Hmm, lemme check on my buddy's cigar here," he said. "I wanna make sure I gave Ron the same fine cigar we're both enjoying, the Libertad Robusto. Lemme see."

The Latina smiled at him. Owens sat in Adams's chair and picked up the cigar Adams had been smoking. He turned around and made sure his back was toward the Latina, blocking her view, blocking anyone's view, actually.

"Oh, yeah." He brought the cigar close to his eyes. "I think it's the same brand. Different label, but same cigar. I carry different brands with me, you know. Lemme see."

With the cigar in his left hand, Owens reached into his right pants pocket and pulled out small tweezers and a tiny vial. It took him all of seven seconds to peel a small cigar section containing Adams's saliva, place that section in the tiny glass tube, and cap and store the small tube back in his pocket.

"Yes. Good. It's the La Libertad Robusto."

CHAPTER NINETEEN

It was a Saturday morning at the Camp Liberty TDS office outside of Baghdad. Sanders had been boots on the ground there for exactly a week. He had just finished a consultation with a soldier-client facing an administrative separation from the army for smoking spice—synthetic marijuana, a prohibited substance. Now he was checking his e-mail notices. He saw: "Hello from CPT Jacob Epstein" and "Owens Update." He double-clicked on Jacob's e-mail.

> Mark, buddy. How goes the war in the big sandbox called Iraq? Things here are fine. Lots of cases, lots of construction. Starbucks, some restaurants, including Buffalo Wild Wings—all under construction. Everyone here says hello. Anything I can do for you? Need anything? Goodies? Books? Cookies? Care Packages? Anything? When are you planning on taking your R&R vacation? How's Lisa? Oh, any new developments in the Adams case? Don't blow too much

money on that one; I still think he's guilty.
Stay safe.

Best.
Government Hack, Jacob

Sanders hit the reply button.

Hi, Jacob. Things are well here. Busy
office, but not as busy as Fort Bliss. Fewer
court-martials, but more Article 15s and
administrative separations. We've got
everything here, so I really don't need
anything, but thanks for offering. Great
mess halls and plenty of food here. MWR
offices have plenty of books too, and they
host poker nights! Great team here, like at
Bliss. I work with great JAG officers and
paralegals. Send my best to everyone.

Lisa's doing well. I call every night. I'm
planning on taking my two-week R&R
in late December around Christmastime;
I want to take Lisa skiing in Colorado. If
you see Lisa, tell her everything is fine,
but between you and me (don't share this
with her), we do get rocketed with enemy
fire here regularly. It is a combat zone. I
don't want Lisa to worry unnecessarily.
We've got plenty of bunkers, and there's an
efficient warning system letting us know
when enemy fire is coming our way. No

new developments in the Adams case, but
I just received an e-mail from Owens that
I haven't checked yet. I'll keep you posted.

True Believer, Mark

He hit the send button. He then double-clicked on
the e-mail from Owens.

> CPT Sanders, two hours ago, I was
> able to track down Ronald Adams and get
> a DNA sample from him. I will FedEx
> the sample to Dr. Robertson's office in
> Cleveland. I need another two grand. This
> evening, I will assess our case and give you
> an update in 24–48 hours. Do you give me
> the okay to charge your credit card for the
> expenses?
> Sincerely, Dale Owens

Sanders hit the reply button and typed the following:

> Thank you, Mr. Owens. You have my
> credit card information, and yes, I give you
> permission to charge the two thousand
> dollars for the expenses. I look forward to
> your update.

CHAPTER TWENTY

"Hey, babe. You doing okay?"

"Hey, Mark. Gosh, you sound like you're right next to me. Thanks for calling."

"Yeah, we have great phones here."

"What time is it in Iraq again?"

"We're ten hours ahead of you. It's 10:00 p.m. here."

"Oh, okay."

"Everything fine, honey?"

"Yeah," Lisa replied.

"How's yoga going?"

"Great, actually. I should be certified by the time you visit for Christmas."

"That's awesome."

"Yeah. Hey, honey, we got mail today, including a package from Dr. Robertson."

"Cool. Great," Sanders said. "What does he say?"

"I don't know. I haven't opened it."

"Please open it up, babe, and read it to me."

"Okay. Let me get the package."

Roughly two minutes passed, and Lisa was back on the phone.

"Okay, lemme open it up … there. Uh, there're some charts here, uh … and a report—"

"Read me the report, babe."

Lisa started reading the report, but it was technical stuff that Sanders couldn't piece together: sequence adenine, cytosine, guanine, thymine, loci matches, slippage.

"Honey, it also says 'LRs: likelihood ratios.'"

"Honey, does Dr. Robertson have a finding or conclusion or executive summary in his report?"

"Uh, let's see." She kept going through the report.

"It says 'mixed sample.' That's really all I see: 'mixed sample.'"

"Okay. Thanks, honey. I'll e-mail Dr. Robertson tonight and ask him for an e-mail attachment version."

"It also says that if you need him to testify in court, his fee is two thousand dollars a day plus travel expenses."

"Okay. Thanks, Lisa."

"And you're gonna get Skype, right, so we can Skype?"

"Yes, babe. I'll have Skype in a couple of days."

"I miss you, Mark. Everything okay there? It's not too dangerous, right?"

"Nah. Everything's good, babe. It's safe. Don't worry."

CHAPTER TWENTY-ONE

Owens was in a Motel Six in Phoenix going over the case file. It was a Sunday evening. A half-empty pizza box occupied the right side of the small desk he was hovering over. He was wearing a white T-shirt and blue boxers, and he was drinking a Diet Coke. It wasn't a solid case, in his opinion.

He flipped open his laptop and started typing.

DNA is only so-so. Sanders sent me the report. Mixed sample—nothing new, really, because we already knew that—no complete definitive match. Good I got a piece of cigar, but it doesn't really help us. Army CID, Criminal Investigative Division, did a so-so job. They didn't obtain and preserve evidence too well from the crime scene. We don't have the senior Adams at the scene of the crime; we just know he visited El Paso about a year ago, a period that roughly coincides with the time of the crime. I recorded the conversation at the bar the other night, but there's nothing hugely incriminating. No eyewitnesses saw him at the party. Victim, Ms. Martinez, wouldn't be able to identify him. Sister of Sergeant Adams says she was raped by father, Ronald Adams. Is she credible? Also, even if he did rape her, it doesn't mean he raped Martinez.

He reached over and picked up a slice of pepperoni pizza. He took a bite.

Christ, man, he thought as he sipped from his Diet Coke. *I don't have a good feeling on this one; we don't have enough. Mixed sample simply shows Martinez had sex with more than one person that night.*

He decided to do a set of push-ups. *I always think better after doing push-ups.*

He did forty push-ups in less than thirty seconds. At six foot three and 230 pounds, Owens was still in excellent shape, but at forty-five, he was nothing like he had been at twenty, when he was a starting linebacker for Clemson. Knee injury after knee injury cut his collegiate football career short. Then came a three-year stint in the army as a military policeman, followed by eight years with the Houston Police Department—two careers that were also hampered by his bad knees. At thirty-three, he found himself tired, worn out, and not happy with the union mandatory health plan that wouldn't pay for the knee surgeon of his choice. His response: *I'll pay for the surgery myself.* His knees did steadily improve after intense rehabilitation, and having an independent and entrepreneurial bug in him, he struck out on his own and started his own private investigative firm: Dale Owens,

Private Investigator LLC. Missing persons was a big part of his practice, but the bulk of his work involved snooping around estranged husbands who allegedly cheated on their wives—work that often meant he had to testify in family courts.

He sat back in the swivel chair and stared at what he had recently typed:

> DNA weak; daughter credible? Martinez? We don't even have Adams at the scene of the crime.

He took a sip of Diet Coke.
Christ, man, I gotta go for it.
He knew what he had to do.

CHAPTER TWENTY-TWO

"Ron Adams, please."

"Just a minute, sir."

It was Monday morning, and Owens had just called Doug's Garage.

"Ron Adams."

"Ron, my brother. Bob Foster here. Got a minute?"

"Sure. And thanks for the beers and cigar the other night."

"Sure. Hey, listen, my man, got a job for you. Can we meet somewhere to discuss?"

At 11:00 a.m. sharp, Owens met Adams at the same O'Brien's Pub where they had met three nights before.

"Beer, Ron?"

"Nah, I'm good."

"Iced tea?"

"Sure."

"Bartender, two iced teas, please."

"Sweetened or unsweetened?" asked the bartender, a petite brunette with an assortment of tattoos on her right arm.

"Ron, how do you like your tea?"

"Sweetened."

"Make it two sweetened iced teas, darling."

Owens cleared his throat, and then he got right to the point. No one was in the bar except them and the petite bartender.

"I need you to drive my hauler truck to El Paso. Only hauling an old Mercedes. The old car will be carrying some stuff of importance—if you know what I mean. I'll give you the El Paso address, and all you have to do is park the truck with the car on the flatbed. Somebody will see you and give you a ride back to Phoenix, 'cause we's got other deals going from here. El Paso's about a five-hour drive. If we get going at noon, you're back home around 10:00 p.m., and you're three grand richer. What you say?"

Adams's eyes lightened up, and he mustered, "I figured you was dealing."

"What you say, Ron? A cool three grand. Just tell your boss you're sick and you're taking the rest of the day off."

"Two iced teas, gentlemen," said the bartender. She placed the glasses in front of them.

"Thanks," said Owens as he placed a ten-dollar bill on the bar. He then looked at Adams. "Look, brother, we all have to cut a living. My kids turned out all right, but they didn't come cheap. Plus, I gotta pay my ex-wife alimony. And like you, I'm dating a hot Latina. Cute babe in El Paso. Gorgeous chica, but she don't come cheap neither. Shit, man, when I take her out to eat, I have to take like her whole extended family out and shit: mother, aunt, sister, cousins, a whole crew. Yunno the deal."

Adams smiled.

"What you say, Ron? An easy three grand, brother. Half up front. It's a two-man job. I'll be driving my car behind you as a lookout. A small load of coke. No biggie. Too easy, my man."

Adams sipped some of his iced tea.

"Why can't you drive the truck?"

"Like I said, my brother, it's a two-man job. I need someone I can trust. I trust you, brother. My regular runner here moved to Denver—late notice and all. What you say? We got a deal?"

CHAPTER TWENTY-THREE

Owens met Adams in the parking lot of the Motel Six.

"Here you go, brother. Keys to that truck right over there."

Adams saw the blue hauler truck; an old, tan Mercedes was chained atop the truck's flatbed.

"You good with the directions?"

"Good," said Adams, nodding his head approvingly.

Owens reached inside his sport jacket and pulled out a white envelope. He had planned this whole trip the previous night and earlier that morning with assistance from the Phoenix Police Department.

"There are fifteen Ben Franklins in there. Another fifteen when you park the truck at the warehouse in El Paso. Want me to count 'em?"

"Nah, man. We's good, Bob. I'll count 'em when I'm inside the truck. If there's a problem with your math, I'll let you know."

"Fair enough, brother."

Owens got into his car, a plain, black 2008 Honda Accord with beige interior. He saw Adams walk over to the truck and get inside the truck's cab. Adams revved up the truck and pulled out of the parkway. Owens followed, but not too closely. Ten minutes later, Adams was pulled over by the Phoenix Police.

CHAPTER TWENTY-FOUR

Adams sat in an uncomfortable gray metal chair in a tiny windowless room inside the Phoenix Police Department headquarters. He sat there for nearly a half hour before a detective, Raul Higuera, age forty-nine, started asking him questions.

After fifteen minutes of some back and forth banter and exchanges, Higuera asked if Adams wanted some water or maybe a cup of coffee.

"Yeah, sure," Adams said. "Coffee. Black. I don't know nothing 'bout some coke shipment. I'm just bringing an old car to El Paso, man."

Five minutes later, Higuera came back to the tiny concrete-walled room and handed Adams a small, white Styrofoam cup filled with coffee. Joining him was Detective Smith, a tall thirty-two-year-old with thick, brown hair. Smith was dressed in a dark business suit. His white shirt was perfectly starched, his tie dark blue in color. Smith stood up and started asking questions.

"So, who do you work for? Where are you supposed to drop off this shipment? Why are you carrying fifteen hundred dollars in cash?" On and on, question after question, but Adams remained noncommittal.

We don't want him to request a lawyer, guys, Owens kept thinking as he was listening to all this in a nearby room. Higuera and Smith were now alternating questions, and Adams kept saying, "I don't know nothing."

Suddenly, Owens decided to make his move. He entered the tiny, bugged room.

Adams did the biggest double-take when he saw Owens.

"Well, I'll be damned. Should've known you were blue," he said. "Cop, man. I've been set up by a fucking pig." He took a sip of coffee, and then he smiled and shook his head disapprovingly.

"You boys ain't got nothing on me. Ever hear of entrapment, fellas? I wasn't born yesterday." He laughed out loud.

"We're not here about some drug shipment, Ron," Owens said.

Adams shifted in his chair. A puzzled look overcame him.

"Come again?"

"We're here for something more important."

Adams was silent.

"El Paso, Ron. Last year. Last summer. Son's birthday, man. Remember that?"

Adams frowned.

"Young lady by the name of Sonia Martinez. You raped her, Ron. You know you did."

Silence.

"We'll drop the charges on this drug shipment thing. Hell, maybe you're right—entrapment and shit. But I wouldn't count on it. We'll drop it, Ron, but we want to know about the rape."

Adams shifted in his chair. He said nothing.

"Ron, we know you did it. We know this."

Silence.

"Ron, buddy. Brother, come clean with us. Save yourself, man."

Silence.

"You need to tell us what happened, Ron."

Silence.

Owens rubbed his chin. "We've got not one but *two* eyewitnesses, Ron," Owens said, lying. "They told me they saw you at that party."

Silence.

"Ron, brother, your own son is doing hard time at Leavenworth, man. For something he didn't do. Save him, Ron. Save your own son. Be a man, brother."

Silence.

"Ron, we know it all. It's game over, brother, game over. Save yourself, man. Just tell us what happened, and we'll give you a light sentence." Smith and Higuera, both standing with their arms crossed, nodded in approval.

"Save yourself and save your son, Keyshawn," Owens said. He was sitting in a chair directly across from Adams, just three feet away from him.

Silence.

"Ron, it's a done deal. I'm telling you. Two eyewitnesses. We know it all; we have it all. What else do you want to know? Did I mention DNA, Ron?"

Adams shifted in his chair.

"Brother, we've got fucking *D* fucking *N* fucking *A* on you. I'm trying to help you here, Ron."

Adams again shifted in his seat. His head was down, and he kept his eyes fixed on the brown, shiny concrete floor.

"Yeah, this drug shipment thing is all bullshit. Don't worry 'bout that. But rape, Ron. C'mon, now. We know it all. Tell us what happened."

Adams again shifted in his chair. His face was sad.

"We know you did it. You know you did it. Ron, you hit that girl so hard you broke her jaw, man. And now your son—your own flesh and blood—is in jail for something he didn't do."

Silence.

"Court-martial got it wrong, Ron. You got lucky. But we ran the DNA again, and we reinterviewed all the witnesses. Two said they saw you there. Your DNA was on that girl."

Silence.

"Ron, brother, I'm telling you, save yourself. Come clean with us, otherwise, we'll throw the whole book on you. Some one hundred years in jail—life in jail, buddy."

Silence, but Adams again shifted in his chair.

"Tell us what happened, Ron. Tell us, brother."

Silence.

"How could you, Ron? Your own son, man. Doing hard time in Leavenworth. Ron, I'm telling you, and I'm serious: tell us what happened, and we'll get you a light sentence." Higuera and Smith again nodded approvingly.

"Save yourself and your son, Ron. Save two people here."

Silence.

Fuck it, Owens thought. He only had one more bullet to fire.

"Ron, Ron. Listen to me. Look at me, brother."

Adams kept his head down and said nothing. He again shifted in his chair.

"Ron, we know it all. And we have all the evidence we need."

Silence.

"Okay, Ron, I gotta tell ya. There's something else we know. See, I've been telling you we know it all. You know you raped Sonia Martinez."

Silence.

"See, Ron, we know you raped someone else too."

Adams shifted in his chair.

"That's right, we know this. Two rapes, Ron. Come clean with us on the Martinez rape, and all the other stuff goes away."

Adams suddenly coughed and sniffed, but he said nothing, and he kept looking at the floor.

"Look at me, Ron. Look at me, brother."

Adams didn't budge.

"Ron, we know everything about the Martinez rape, and we know you did it. We also know everything about the other rape."

Silence.

"Your own daughter, Ron," Owens said softly. "That's right. We know everything about that one too."

Adams's body suddenly started trembling.

"You have two kids, Ron. Your own flesh and blood, brother. And you screwed up both of their lives. But you can redeem yourself, brother."

Adams said nothing, but his entire body kept trembling.

"Yeah, two beautiful kids, Ron. I met them both," Owens said, lying. "You can fix everything, Ron. Tell us what happened in the Martinez rape, and we'll drop everything else."

Adams shook his head disapprovingly; his body kept trembling.

"Your son's in jail, Ron. And your daughter, when she was just fourteen, was raped by you. Ron, brother, just come to Jesus, man. Just tell us what happened and we'll——"

"Okay, okay," Adams said in a low voice while still looking at the floor.

"What's that, Ron? I didn't hear you."

"Okay. I raped the girl in El Paso."

CHAPTER TWENTY-FIVE

"Hey, there's the man."

Sanders and Epstein hugged each other.

"On the big R&R. How goes the deployment?"

"Can't complain. Living the dream."

The two were at the German Club at Fort Bliss. They were standing at the bar next to other patrons. Sanders's two-week rest-and-relaxation deployment vacation had started two days ago. Tomorrow, he would be on a flight to Colorado for some skiing with Lisa.

"What do you want to drink, Mark?"

"I'll have the German lager on draft."

"Sure thing."

"Bartender, two lagers on draft, please. We're starting a tab."

Jacob slapped Mark on the back as the two walked over to a nearby table. "It's great to see you, buddy," he said as the two sat down. "I was thinking Buffalo Wild Wings would be operating on post by now, but they've had some construction delays on account of the weather."

"Bliss just continues to grow, huh?" Mark said. "It's changed a lot in the three months I've been away."

The two continued to catch up, and some five minutes later, the waitress came over to their table and placed two filled beer mugs in front of them.

"Cheers, buddy," Jacob said, to which Mark replied, "Cheers." They touched mugs.

"I gotta tell you, Mark, awesome job on the Adams case."

"Thanks. Owens really paid off. He deserves all the credit."

"I was wrong, Mark, and you were right."

"Well, I wasn't sure," Mark said, "but we decided to probe and take a chance. Nothing like a confession from the suspect. Again, Owens deserves the credit."

The two sipped from their beer mugs, and then Jacob suddenly reached into the left inside pocket of his brown leather jacket and pulled out a clipped newspaper article.

"See this morning's *El Paso Times*?"

"Nope, but Lisa told me there was an online story that ran two days ago. Sergeant Adams is gonna get a retrial."

"Yeah, that's right."

"Hey, Lisa's pregnant, by the way."

"Ah, Mark, that's awesome, man. I'm happy for you both."

"Thanks. We're happy."

"Hey, take a look at the article I just placed on the table."

Sanders looked at the article in front of him.

District Attorney to Prosecute Rape Case
Exonerates Soldier—Father Is Suspect

EL PASO—District Attorney Carlos Jimenez announced yesterday that the city will prosecute Ronald Adams, 44, of Phoenix, for the 2009 rape of Sonia Martinez, 25. Adams's son, Sergeant Keyshawn Adams, 25, a soldier formerly stationed at Fort Bliss, is currently serving a 25-year prison term at the US Disciplinary Barracks at Leavenworth, Kansas, for the rape.

In a separate statement, Jimenez said he had negotiated with the Army Court of Criminal Appeals (ACCA) to see to it that the younger Adams receive a court-martial retrial. Jimenez said the negotiated retrial practically guarantees the exoneration of Sergeant Adams because …

"Good stuff," Sanders said. He took a sip of beer.

"Mark, man, you did it. I propose two toasts," Jacob said. "To Lisa's pregnancy," he said loudly.

"To Lisa's pregnancy," Mark said. Their mugs touched.

"And to the True Believers."

"To the True Believers."

Printed in the United States
By Bookmasters